Magic Pony

Nighttime Adventure

Show jumping by moonlight! What could be more thrilling?

"Penelope Potter'd be furious if she found out I'd used her jumps without asking," whispered Annie, and with shining eyes she took hold of the reins and sprang onto Ned's back. Rain boots and pajamas disappeared and she was transformed into a rider with velvet riding hat, hacking jacket, jodhpurs, and jodhpur boots.

"Penelope Potter will never ever find out," Ned whispered back.

**Join Annie on all her adventures
with Ned, the Magic Pony!**

Magic Pony
Nighttime Adventure

Elizabeth Lindsay

Illustrated by John Eastwood

SCHOLASTIC INC.

For my uncle, R.W.H., with love.

ISBN 978-0-545-57646-8

Text copyright © 1997 by Elizabeth Lindsay.
Illustrations copyright © 1997 by John Eastwood.
All rights reserved. Published by Scholastic Inc.,
557 Broadway, New York, NY 10012, by arrangement with
Scholastic Children's Books, Scholastic Ltd.
SCHOLASTIC and associated logos are trademarks
and/or registered trademarks of Scholastic Inc.

12 11 10 9 8 7 6 5 4 3 2 1   13 14 15 16 17 18/0

Printed in the U.S.A.   40

This edition first printing, January 2013

Chapter 1

Nighttime Surprise

Annie woke up suddenly and unexpectedly. Something in the dark was tickling her ear. It felt like the hairy feet of a spider and she quickly brushed it away. The tickling started again on her chin and warm air blew on her cheek. Pressing herself against the wall, she reached the light switch at last. She laughed when the light came on. It wasn't a spider at all. Not even close. It was the tickling of pony whiskers and the blowing of warm pony breath. Ned, the beautiful chestnut pony who lived in the poster pinned to her bedroom wall, had wakened her. His gentle lips nuzzled affectionately against her cheek. How lucky she was to have such a secret: her very own magic pony. She rubbed the sleep from her eyes and glanced at the clock on the shelf.

"Hello," said the pony cheerfully, not seeming to mind that he only just fit into the space between the bed and the wall.

"Ned," said Annie. "It's two-thirty in the morning. Why aren't you asleep?"

"Now what sort of greeting is that?" asked the pony. "Do you want me to go back in my poster?"

"No," said Annie, alarmed that he might. Ever since buying this most unusual pony poster from Cosby's Magic Emporium, Annie never quite knew when Ned would come alive. If the magic was happening now, she didn't want to waste a moment of it. "It's only that it's the middle of the night. I've never been awake at two-thirty in the morning before."

"That's the whole point," said Ned. "Everyone in the house is fast asleep, even that cat."

Ned meant Tabitha, Annie's tabby cat, who lay curled up on the bed. This wasn't quite true, for Annie's wriggling had disturbed her, and Tabitha had half an eye open. As for Ned, whether big or small — and he could be either — Tabitha had learned to ignore him.

"It's the perfect time for jumping practice. So get up and get on."

During the day, when her curtains were open, Annie often watched Penelope Potter jump her pony, Pebbles, over the blue barrels in the field on the other side of the road. And now Ned was teaching her to do the same! What did it matter if it was the middle of the night? Annie scrambled out from under the covers, leaving Tabitha to curl up into an undisturbed ball.

"I can't ride in pajamas. I'd better get my jeans on."

"No need for that," said Ned. And of course there wasn't, for the moment Annie sat on Ned's back, the magic would change her pajamas into riding clothes.

"Where shall we jump?" Annie asked, putting her bare toes into the waiting stirrup and springing on. The pony's reply was drowned out in a rushing wind, and Annie closed her eyes. When she opened

them again, Ned was trotting across a field of brown tufts that Annie recognized as her carpet. Ned's magic had shrunk them into the tiniest pony and tiniest rider in the world. He rounded the towering height of the door and cantered toward the top of the stairs, guided by the light that spilled from Annie's bedroom.

"Where are we going?" Annie whispered.

"Downstairs, of course," came the reply.

The drop from the landing onto the first stair was huge and the giant steps disappeared into a pit of black. Jumping practice was starting in earnest. Annie clung on, remembering she had gone downstairs like this before. By the time they reached the hall, Annie's eyes were staring pools, desperate to fathom what lay ahead in the darkness. To her relief, she hadn't fallen off. Just as well! Any loud noise would wake Mom, Dad, and Jamie, and she certainly didn't want that.

"Get off now," said Ned. "And switch on the dining room light. We'll set up a jumping course in there."

"Oh, yes," said Annie. "I know the very best place." She slid to the ground and let go of the reins. The wind spun her until she was her correct size and back in her pajamas. She tiptoed forward, following the tiny Ned. He cantered in front of her as if he were Esmerelda, Prince, or Percy, one of her three china horses, come to life. She pushed open the dining room door and switched on the light. Fred, the goldfish, fluttered into action in his bowl on the shelf, surprised by the sudden brightness. Annie hurried to the table. It was already set for breakfast, just the way Mom liked it.

"Ned, let's make a jumping course up here. There's lots of things that could be jumps."

"Show me." Annie held out her hand and lifted him. Ned was soon trotting across the tablecloth, inspecting the breakfast dishes.

"Yes," he said. "The syrup bottle, the knives and forks, and the salt and pepper shakers. We can use all those."

"And the mugs," said Annie. "They can lie on their sides and be pretend barrels. Almost as good as the barrels Penelope Potter has for Pebbles to jump."

"They'll make a mighty jump, mind you," said Ned, trotting around one. "The plates are no use. They need to be put off to one side."

"My schoolbag's here," said Annie grabbing it from beside a chair and diving in. "My pens and pencils can be poles."

She scattered three felt-tips and two striped pencils on the table and pulled out her scissors. "What can my scissors be? I know, they can be opened out and balanced on their handles. They're not sharp, so there's no chance of getting cut. They'll make a great cross-blade jump. And look, Mom's sewing basket is loaded with spools of thread. They can be jump stands."

"Good thinking," said Ned. "As our small selves we'll practice indoors on the table, and as our large selves we'll ride out to Penelope Potter's field and jump Pebbles's barrels."

"In the dark?" exclaimed Annie, already balancing a knife and a fork across the salt and pepper shakers.

"It's a full moon tonight," said Ned. "With luck, we'll have plenty of light."

Annie darted to the window and pulled back the curtains, knowing Penelope would hate someone else jumping her blue barrels, even if it was in the dark. So she wouldn't find out. Annie shielded her eyes and looked into the garden. Through a gap in the ballooning clouds, a round moon flooded silver light across the grass.

"If the clouds clear away, it'll be perfect," Annie said, looking for stars.

How exciting it would be to do nighttime jumping outdoors. She returned to the table.

After the salt-and-pepper shaker–knife-and-fork jump, she opened the scissors and balanced them on their handles to make the cross-blade jump. The mugs were put on their sides and turned into barrels, and the spools of thread were stacked at three different heights. Two of the pens and one of the pencils became poles, making the pen and pencil staircase.

Next she turned the syrup bottle on its side to make a wall. And finally, Annie discovered Mom's glasses in the sewing basket, opened them out, and made three jumps. The eyeglasses single, if jumped facing the lenses, or the eyeglasses double, if the arms were jumped. She bounced over them with her fingers — *boing! boing!* Then she watched enchanted as Ned, mane flying, jumped the whole course.

It was a clear round and Annie clasped her hands to stop herself from clapping — a thing certain to wake the family and bring them downstairs to find out what was going on. Instead, her delight was shown by a grin that grew wider and wider as Ned trotted toward her. Leaning back on his haunches, he bowed politely.

"Now it's your turn, Annie. I'll come down to the floor, then you can mount. But we'll need some sort of road to ride up, to get us back up here as our small selves."

"I know," said Annie. "If I pull Dad's chair close to the table, we can use the rug."

She hurried to show Ned what she meant. After a bit of a struggle, she had the chair in position with the rug draped over it. One end hung from the chair back while Annie stretched the other end out over the seat and weighted it with the legs of the small table. Now there was a long ramp from the floor to the top of the chair.

"Well done," said Ned, impressed. He jumped onto the rug and galloped all the way down to the floor without causing the slightest sag.

When his feet touched the floor, he was suddenly his big self, wearing saddle and bridle and filling a large part of the room. Annie squeezed between Ned and the table and took hold of the reins.

The moment she sprang into the saddle, the mighty wind blew. When it stopped, she was dressed in her magic riding clothes and was dwarfed by giant furniture. As she looked up, her breath was taken away by the vast chair and rug mountain. Ned stepped onto the rug ramp cautiously, but Annie's extra weight made no difference; the rug stayed taut and stretched. The pony trotted briskly all the way to the top and jumped onto the table.

Annie gasped with surprise at what she saw. As her big self she thought she had made the show jumps sensibly low, but now that she was a tiny rider they looked huge. Most frightening of all were the giant mug barrels — imposingly round and solid and higher than Ned's shoulders.

"This is just the sort of practice course you need," said Ned. "Jump all of these and you'll soon be showing that Penelope Potter what's what."

"Yes," said Annie faintly. It seemed like a flock of butterflies had been let loose in her tummy. Right now she didn't care if Penelope Potter could do show jumping better than she could. She wanted to go back to bed.

"Hold on tight," said Ned. Annie gulped, pulled nervously at the chin strap of her riding hat, then took a rein in each hand. Ned cantered toward the salt-and-pepper shaker–knife-and-fork jump.

It was now or never.

Chapter 2

Things That Go Bump
in the Night

"Here we go," Ned said. At the last moment, Annie grabbed a handful of mane. Ned soared into the air and, leaning into the angle of the jump, Annie went with him. Ned hit the tablecloth on the other side with a thump and was cantering toward the open scissors cross-blade before Annie realized what was happening. The scissors were quickly behind them and Ned turned for the eyeglasses. It seemed strange cantering - toward them. It hardly seemed possible that these glasses, so often perched on Mom's nose, were now as high as the stirrup irons.

"Don't worry about a thing," said Ned. "Just go with the jump." And he leaped. For a moment Annie caught a glimpse of Ned's legs reflected in the lens, then they were in the air and on the other side,

cantering around to the syrup-bottle wall. The syrup bottle seemed like nothing after the eyeglasses, and even the pen and pencil staircase, which came next, was easy. Ned made a tight turn and suddenly the mug barrels lay ahead, by far the biggest jump. The pony gathered himself up, shortening his stride, and the barrels came closer. Annie concentrated hard, and the moment Ned sprang she was ready. Ned cleared the barrels and so did she!

"Well done," he said. Annie was jubilant. It was a clear round.

"I didn't think I could do it, but I did. Thank you, Ned." She leaned forward and gave the pony a hug.

"Now it's your turn to steer," said Ned. "You guide me wherever you want to go."

"All right," said Annie, filled with a glorious sense of accomplishment. "We'll go around again."

So engrossed were they, neither of them noticed the dining room door open just enough for a curious cat to pad silently in. And they didn't see Tabitha slip under

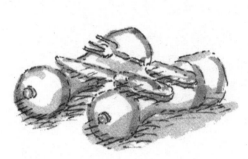

the tablecloth to listen to the unusual thuds coming from above.

Although there was lots to think about, Annie found steering fun, and with mounting excitement she turned Ned toward the salt-and-pepper shaker–knife-and-fork jump. They were quickly over it and cantered toward the scissors, which they cleared easily, and the syrup-bottle wall, which caused no problems either. After this, Annie changed the route and swung Ned around to jump the arms of the eyeglasses. Only when they were facing them did she realize this was going to be trickier than she thought.

It was too late to stop. Ned jumped, hit the tablecloth, and jumped again. But it was too quick for Annie. By the second landing, she had lost her balance. As Ned slowed to help her, the tablecloth suddenly shifted and an unexpected, furry giant landed in front of them.

"Look out!" Ned shouted, swerving sharply. "Get off the table!"

Now nothing could stop Annie, and she and Ned parted company. In a split second, Annie grew to her proper size and landed in the middle of the table. There was a terrible rattling of dishes and all the show jumps collapsed. Tabitha dived for the floor, Ned for the safety of the rug ramp. Unable to stop herself, Annie slid, pulling the tablecloth, breakfast things, and show jumps off the table with her.

The crash and clatter was startling and, landing with a surprised grunt among the debris, Annie sat stunned. Then, from the corner of her eye, she saw the alarmed Fred swimming around and around in his bowl.

"Sorry Fred," she said. "No need to panic." Then she realized that, after a crash like that, there was *every* need to panic. She looked around quickly for Ned. Both he and Tabitha had disappeared. *Just as well*, she thought. Mindful that she had bare feet, she unwrapped herself from the tablecloth and hurriedly surveyed the damage.

It wasn't as bad as she expected. One plate was broken in half, there was an open green felt-tip marker on the tablecloth, and the handle of her own special mug had snapped off. The rest was a mess that just needed to be picked up. She started at once. With luck, she could have the table set again before the mess was discovered. Working quickly, she started to pile up the plates and didn't see the tall, slow-moving figure creep in from the hall — with a big, black boot held up as a ready defense.

"Annie! What do you think you're doing?"

She nearly jumped out of her skin.

"Dad!" Behind Dad was Jamie, pale and wide-eyed, brandishing the magic wand from his conjuring set. "You really frightened me!" she said with a gasp.

"*Us* frighten *you*? What sort of a fright do you think you gave us? We thought you were a burglar. Your mother's under the covers, shaking with fear," said Dad.

"No, I'm not," said Mom. "I just had to get my robe on." Even Mom was clasping a wooden coat hanger to her chest. "I couldn't meet a burglar in my nightie."

"Oh," said Annie.

"Yes," said Jamie. "We were going to tie you up and hand you over to the police."

"Humph!" said Dad, dropping the boot in the hall. "That won't be necessary now that we know it was you."

"I'm sorry I woke you," said Annie. "I

had a little accident with the tablecloth. Well, it was Tabitha. She got on the table and, well, her claws pulled it and, well, everything came off." It was the closest to the truth she could manage, and Annie hoped that it would do.

"But what were you doing down here at this time of night?" Dad asked. "It's after three o'clock. You should be fast asleep." Annie held up her broken mug with one hand and crossed her fingers behind her back with the other.

"I came to get a mug of water and now I've broken it. Sorry."

Fortunately, Tabitha chose this moment to come out from behind the sofa and brush herself against Annie's legs.

"Honestly, that cat's more trouble than she's worth," said Mom. "Come on, we can leave the mess until morning. Back to bed everyone."

But Annie realized she couldn't leave everything until the morning. There were pens and pencils, spools of thread and scissors mixed in with the dishes. She needed to put them away to avoid anyone asking any more awkward questions.

"Leave everything." Mom was firm. "Find a mug with a handle and fill it. Then it's straight up to bed."

Dad shook his head. "Accidents will happen, I suppose," he said. "Excitement's over, Jamie. Back to bed now. It's a school day tomorrow."

When Annie came from the kitchen carrying her water, she looked around quickly for Ned. He was nowhere to be seen, thank goodness, although she longed to know where he'd gone. Mom's hand on her shoulder steered her out of the dining room.

"Can we leave the door open for Tabitha?" Annie asked.

"I suppose so," said Mom, switching off the light. "Now upstairs at once. In the future, remember to take water up with you when you go to bed. We don't want a repeat performance of tonight, thank you very much."

Annie plodded up the stairs with her mug clasped in both hands. She stopped at the top.

"If I was a burglar, would you have bashed me with the coat hanger?"

With twinkling eyes, Mom waved it.

"If you'd been stealing my favorite flower vase — yes! Now hurry back to bed."

Annie hurried into her bedroom and checked to see if Ned was back in his poster. He wasn't. She put the mug beside her clock, flopped onto the bed with a sigh, and switched off the light. *It's lucky*

Mom and Dad don't seem upset so far, she thought. But the kind of accident they *think* I've had is one thing. Show jumping on the table is quite another. If they find *that* out, then they'll be mad. She covered her knees with the blanket.

When everyone had gone back to sleep, she would find Ned and sort out the show jumps from the rest of the dishes on the floor.

Chapter 3

The Moon Shines Bright

It was difficult trying to stay awake. Annie propped herself against the wall, but soon her head nodded forward. When her chin knocked her chest, she opened her eyes and shook herself, but the effect didn't last long. Her eyelids drooped and down went her chin again. This time she didn't wake up.

It was Tabitha landing on the bed, purring loudly and brushing her body against Annie's sagging knees that finally woke her.

"Mmm, mmm, what?" Slowly she awoke. "Tabby?" she said and wrapped her arms around the warm furry bundle. The purring grew even louder. Annie would have dropped off again if Tabitha hadn't licked the back of her hand. The rasping sound and prickly sensation woke her completely, and, remembering what she had to do, she felt along the shelf for her little flashlight.

"This time, Tabby, you stay here," whispered Annie. She shone the flashlight beam on the clock. A quarter to four! Then onto Ned's poster. Empty. She listened hard and, although Tabitha was still purring, the rest of the house seemed quiet and still. Cautiously, she climbed out of bed, tiptoed to the window, and lifted back the curtain. The sky was full of stars, and the field on the other side of the road was flooded with moonlight.

Esmerelda, Prince, and Percy stood in a line on the windowsill. They seemed to stare at the spot where Penelope Potter's pony, Pebbles, stood. With his head up and ears pricked, he was a shining silver statue in the middle of a silver lake. Annie craned her neck to see what he was

looking at. Whatever it was, it was way out of view, and she didn't dare open the window in case it made a noise.

She let the curtain fall; she had important things to do. She squeezed around her bedroom door, and, turning the handle bit by bit, closed it without a sound, leaving Tabitha shut in. The flashlight lit her way along the landing and down the stairs.

Annie paused at the bottom and listened. Silence! More confident, she tiptoed into the dining room. She pushed the door open and turned on the light to see the tiny Ned canter across the carpet toward her.

"Are you ready to jump in Pebbles's field?" he asked. "The moon shines bright."

Annie longed to say yes, longed to ride out into the shimmering world of Pebbles's field, but first things first.

"I can't," she said. "Not until I've cleaned up the jumping things."

She put her flashlight in her pajama bottoms pocket and started her search among the wreckage. She closed the scissors, grateful that she hadn't sat on them, and found Mom's glasses in one piece, which was a relief. She picked up the spools of thread and neatly replaced them in Mom's sewing basket, and she shoved the pens and pencils into her schoolbag. There was nothing she could do about the green smudge of felt-tip ink on the tablecloth, but it wasn't a very big smudge, so with luck no one would notice it.

"There," said Annie. "All done. I'll have to leave the silverware and other stuff on the floor, otherwise it'll be obvious I got up again. It's lucky no one noticed the rug over the chair. I never could have explained that." She carefully replaced it on the floor and pulled Dad's chair back into place.

"It was unfortunate about that cat," said Ned. "The jumping was going well until she arrived."

"Never mind," said Annie. "She can't follow us this time. I've shut her up in my bedroom."

"Good," said Ned. "You'd better put something on your feet."

"My boots! They're by the back door. Let's go out that way and around by the side gate."

Annie switched out the light and, with the flashlight, lit the way to the kitchen. There she pulled on her rain-boots and unlocked the back door. The tiny pony jumped from the step, and Annie followed him out into the night.

Nothing stirred. A barn owl hooted in Winchway Wood, and above them twinkled a million distant stars. But most enchanting of all, Annie thought, was seeing Ned standing before her on the grass, a correct-sized pony, tacked up and ready for her to mount. Show jumping by moonlight! What could be more thrilling?

"Penelope Potter'd be furious if she found out I'd used her jumps without asking," whispered Annie, and with shining eyes she took hold of the reins and sprang onto Ned's back. Rain boots and pajamas disappeared and she was transformed into a rider with velvet riding hat, hacking jacket, jodhpurs, and jodhpur boots.

"Penelope Potter will never ever find out," Ned whispered back.

How silly to think that, in such wonderful clothes and riding such a handsome chestnut pony, Penelope Potter even had a chance of recognizing her. Of courses she didn't.

Annie chuckled with excitement as Ned walked across the grass and around the side of the house to the gate. She leaned forward and lifted the latch. Ned backed away so she could pull the gate open, and then they were in the road.

"Ready to go?" asked Ned.

Annie was ready for anything, which was just as well. For, instead of letting Annie open the field gate, Ned trotted a little way down the road, turned and cantered straight for it. He made a huge leap, and they were in the field before the gasp of surprise had left Annie's lips.

"Well sat," said Ned. "In spite of that unfortunate tumble earlier, I can see that you haven't lost your nerve."

"You didn't give me a chance to think about it," said Annie. "After the gate, jumping Pebbles's barrels will be nothing." And her eyes searched the field for the dappled gray pony. "That's funny. Where *is* Pebbles? He was here a little while ago. I saw him from my window."

"Well, he's not here now," said Ned.

With a jolt, Annie remembered Pebbles's fixed look in the direction of Penelope's stable yard and felt a sudden stab of anxiety.

Through the still night air, from the direction of the yard, came the long, lonely whinny of a confused and worried pony. It was answered by a voice Annie had never heard before. Its low, cross tones struck a chill in her heart. She could just make out the words.

"Get on in, horse, or else you'll regret it."

Chapter 4

Thieves in the Night

Above the stable roof, the moonlight lit up the flat top of a horse trailer. Annie froze with fear, but Ned hurried into action and she clung on.

"Don't say a word," he whispered, and, keeping in the shadow of the hedge, they trotted toward Penelope's stable yard. Ned's unshod feet swished through the grass, beating out a soft rhythm. From the yard came the hollow clatter of pony feet climbing up a horse trailer's ramp. Annie recognized the sound from when Penelope loaded Pebbles into his pony trailer, only this time it *wasn't* Penelope. Penelope was tucked in bed, fast asleep. Someone else was loading Pebbles — someone up to no good.

"We've got to stop them," she whispered in Ned's ear. "They're stealing Pebbles!"

"Don't worry," Ned whispered back. "We will." And he broke into a steady canter, charging through the open gate into the stable yard, where he galloped - toward the trailer and straight into a rushing wind. Ned and Annie went from big to small in a moment and disappeared between the front wheels of the trailer just as a pair of trousered legs ran alongside it.

"What was that?" The cross voice again. "I swear there was only one pony in the field. Was that another?"

Now a younger voice.

"No, boss, I didn't see anything."

"Close up the ramp and get in the cab. We have to clear out of here. That gray horse has made enough noise to wake the dead."

One pair of legs disappeared toward the front of the trailer, the other pair ran for the back. Ned galloped from between the rear wheels, swung around and jumped onto the ramp. Up he galloped, leaping each antislip bar like a racehorse, his rider bent double like a jockey. Annie glanced over her shoulder in time to see the thief's accomplice start lifting the ramp.

The ramp straightened under them and Ned half jumped, half fell into the trailer. It banged as it closed behind them, and they were left in pitch blackness. Pebbles, upset by the rough treatment he had received, cried out with an earsplitting whinny that only faded when the engine broke into a roar. The trailer swung out of the yard and drove off, nearly knocking Ned from his feet.

"Annie, are you all right?" Ned asked, his sides heaving as he regained his breath.

"Yes, but I can't see a thing." Wondering if her flashlight would have transferred itself from her pajamas to her jodhpurs, she fumbled in the little pocket near the waistband. What a relief to find it was there!

"Shine it ahead," said Ned. "I need to see where Pebbles's hooves are."

The wobbly pinprick of light picked out Pebbles's four great hooves, one after the other, helping Ned to make his way shakily across the shuddering rubber matting.

"Got my bearings now," said Ned. "Hold tight and crouch right down."

A whirl of wind spun them and, in a moment, Ned was as big as Pebbles and Annie found herself ducking down just below the trailer's roof. Pebbles peered into the flashlight with a look of surprise.

"It's all right, Pebbles. It's only us," said Annie. "I'm going to get off Ned and untie you." Pebbles whickered with relief — friends had arrived.

"Easy does it, Annie," said Ned. "And keep hold of my reins." Annie slid to the ground between the two ponies, who now stood side by side. She looped Ned's reins over her arm and edged toward Pebbles's head. Ned rested his muzzle in a comforting way on the gray pony's neck while Annie untied the halter rope. As soon as he could, Pebbles nuzzled Annie's arm before turning to Ned. The two ponies

blew a nose-to-nose greeting the way
that horses do.

"Now what?" asked Annie, grabbing a handful of Ned's mane as the trailer lurched around a bend.

"We get the thieves to stop," said Ned. "And we do it like this."

To Annie's surprise, Ned's back end lifted into the air and both hind legs kicked hard against the side of the trailer.

Everything swayed. As if this was his cue, Pebbles did the same and to greater effect, because he wore metal horseshoes. The trailer jerked and swayed, and Annie held tight to the tying-up ring. Bang and bang and bang went four pony feet. The metal kicking-plate buckled and above it the wood splintered. There were angry shouts from the driver's cab. The ponies renewed their efforts. Gasping and puffing, they put all their energy into knocking out a big hole.

The trailer came to a spluttering, lurching stop, and the floor ended up angled to one side.

"Looks like we've ended up in a ditch," said Ned cheerfully, as if he couldn't have wished for anything better. "Get on, Annie, and get ready to lead Pebbles down the ramp."

Meanwhile, Pebbles kept up the kicking with one leg, needing his other three to balance. Annie had just enough space. It was the first time she had mounted from this side, and using her right foot was awkward until she got a boost from underneath by Ned's nose.

Once in the saddle, she crouched low to avoid hitting her head on the roof. She had a firm hold of Pebbles's lead rope with one hand, the other held tight to Ned's mane. This was the scariest thing she had ever done, and she took a deep breath to quiet her pounding heart.

Bang and bang and bang went Pebbles. Chunks of wood flew, and there were angry shouts at the back of the trailer.

"Get ready," said Ned, turning to face the ramp. "As soon as this thing goes, down we run."

The lock clicked. Bang, bang went Pebbles for good measure. A slit of moonlight appeared, and the ramp started to go down. Pebbles got in two more kicks, and Ned coiled under Annie like a spring.

"All right, horse," said a brawny

figure, springing toward them. "You asked
for it."

"Charge!" yelled Annie at the top of

her voice, and Ned leaped forward. The
astonished horse thief tumbled backward.

Annie had the satisfaction of seeing him splash into the ditch as Ned clattered down the wildly bouncing ramp, followed by an eager Pebbles. Then, with a sound like gunfire, a hinge snapped. The terrified accomplice dived for the safety of the hedge as not one pony but two jumped to safety and cantered off down the moonlit road.

"That's given them something to think about," said Ned. "Stuck in a ditch with the ramp hanging half off. The horse trailer won't be going anywhere like that. It's really stranded."

"Good," grinned the triumphant Annie, holding tight to Pebbles's lead rope. "They won't be stealing any more ponies tonight, that's for sure."

Behind them, furious shouts faded into the distance.

Chapter 5

Mystery Rider

Pebbles's hooves hammered the road's hard surface and mingled with the duller beat of Ned's unshod feet. The farther they raced, the more Annie was sure a beat was missing. But there was nothing wrong with Pebbles — he cantered easily beside her — and Ned was fine, too. In the end, Annie forgot to listen as she tried instead to work out where they were.

The ponies put a good distance between themselves and the stranded thieves before slowing down. Hot and blowing, they stopped for a rest. The moon seemed to shed less light and the sky was paler. Annie wondered how long they had been traveling and how far they had come.

"Well," said Ned. "Where do we go from here?"

"I'm not sure!" Annie tried desperately to find a recognizable landmark, but the moonlit countryside looked so different from how she usually saw it. "We haven't gone past any turns, so we must have come along this road in the trailer. Best to go straight until I figure it out."

The ponies started walking, and the uneven sound from Pebbles's feet — three clops and a pat — became obvious. Annie finally understood the problem.

"Pebbles has lost a shoe!"

"Wrenched off with all that kicking, no doubt," said Ned. "It's lucky he's not lame." But there was no sign of Pebbles limping. On the contrary, he pulled to go forward. Ahead, the moon hung above a line of dark trees, and behind them was a spire.

"I know where we are!" cried Annie, and she realized Pebbles did, too. "Not far from home. This is our village. That's the church."

They set off at a trot, coming onto Main Street, clattering past the shops, the gas station, and the bus stop. All familiar signs of home.

"Here's our road," said Annie. "That's the front entrance to Penelope's house." She pointed to a smart white gate facing onto the main road. "But mostly the Potters use the other entrance. The back driveway that comes out opposite the stable yard. The old stables behind the house are garages now. That's why Pebbles has a new stable in his field."

They swung into the road and Annie had high hopes of being able to turn Pebbles out without anyone seeing them. But the beam of a flashlight suddenly lit up the lane, and two figures emerged from the Potters' back drive.

"Now what are we going to do?" she

whispered. "It's Mr. Potter and Penelope. They've heard us coming."

"Talk your way out of it. You can do it," Ned whispered back.

"What happens if they recognize me?"

"They won't," Ned assured her.

"Excuse me, that's my pony you've got there!" said Penelope, arms outstretched to stop them from passing. "Hand him over."

"That's enough, Penelope. Just leave this to me," said Mr. Potter. "Now, young lady. What are you doing with my daughter's pony, and what, for that matter, are you doing out at this time of night?"

Annie leaned down and dropped Pebbles's halter rope into Penelope's waiting hand. "I was bringing him back. He's been stolen."

"We know that," said Penelope. "I heard him whinnying. I saw the thieves' trailer drive off up the lane."

Mr. Potter looked puzzled.

"How did you find him?" he asked. "The police are out searching right now."

Terrified they'd recognize her voice, Annie's words tumbled out in a rush.

"He escaped from the horse trailer. It's stuck in a ditch with a broken ramp. Turn left at the top of the road and keep going straight till you find it. Tell the police that. Oh, and he's lost a back shoe." Her legs gave Ned a squeeze. "Good-bye." Ned sprang forward.

"Now just a minute, young lady," cried Mr. Potter, but he was distracted by Pebbles trying to go with them. Mr. Potter had to help Penelope hang on tight and, in doing so, neither of them saw Ned turn at Annie's house and jump the side gate. The girl rider and the pony had vanished by the time Pebbles was calm again.

Quickly, Ned reached the backyard and Annie slid from his back.

"Thank you, Ned, for saving Pebbles and for the wonderful indoor show jumping." She gave him a quick hug and let go of the reins. At once she was back in her pajamas and rain boots.

She pushed the back door open. Ned tossed his mane and in a moment was his tiny self, leaping up the doorstep into the house. Annie hurried after him, locking the door and kicking off her boots as she went. She caught up to Ned on the landing, highlighting him in her flashlight's beam as he pranced, waiting for her.

"Good-bye, Annie, until next time." The tiny pony voice was a drift of tinkling bells.

"Good-bye, Ned. It's been the most exciting night of my life!" came her whispered reply. She pushed open her bedroom door and the miniature pony galloped ahead. By the time Annie had

crept inside, Ned was safely back in his poster. She switched off her flashlight. Daylight was creeping between her curtains; it was nearly morning. She wriggled her feet under the sleeping Tabitha and looked up at Ned's picture.

"Night, night, Magic Pony," she

whispered. "I hope the next time will be soon." And she lay down. She sat up again almost at once. "How typical! Penelope didn't even say thank you." Then, with a sigh of exhaustion, she flopped down again.

The next thing she knew she was being shaken awake by Jamie.

"Mom says you've got to get up now," he said. "What's the matter with you? Why didn't you wake up? She's called and called. Now you've missed breakfast."

"Why? What time is it?"

"Quarter to eight!" said Jamie and left her groaning. Annie thought she must be the weariest person in the world. She looked up at Ned in his poster, and slowly the details of last night's adventure came back: show jumping on the table, the mess on the dining room floor, and saving Pebbles. Tabitha slid off the bed, stretched and trotted off to find her breakfast.

Annie staggered out of bed and, after flinging on her school clothes, arrived in the kitchen with enough time to grab her lunch box.

"About time, too, Annie," said Mom, handing it over. "I've put in an extra sandwich for you to eat on the bus. Now hurry."

"Thanks, Mom." Annie grabbed her schoolbag from the dining room and ran.

She turned the corner at the end of the road and saw Penelope talking

excitedly to Jamie by the school bus stop.
For once, he appeared to be listening.

"Amazing," she heard him say as she
drew close. "Hey, Annie, guess what
happened to Pebbles?"

"I'll tell her if you don't mind, Jamie,"
said Penelope. "He *is* my pony."

"What?" asked Annie, pretending not
to know.

"In the middle of the night, he got
stolen!" Before Annie could think how

to react, Penelope went on. "It was weird. We got him back again. But not from the police. From this mystery rider. We heard ponies coming down the lane and there was this girl, very stylish, on a beautiful chestnut, leading Pebbles. She told us where the thieves' trailer was, handed Pebbles over, and vanished! And she was right. The police caught the thieves trying to pull their trailer out of a ditch with a stolen tractor. Only nobody seems to know who she was. Don't you think that's extraordinary?"

Annie blinked and nodded.

"Yes, and another amazing thing. The thieves tried to say they hadn't stolen Pebbles. But the police found his lost shoe in their trailer, and then the thieves got terribly confused about whether they'd stolen one pony or two. All rather strange don't you think?"

Annie opened her mouth to reply, but was saved from having to by the arrival of the school bus. The three of them climbed aboard and Annie sank thankfully into a seat, grateful her secret was safe and delighted the thieves had been caught. Now Penelope had a new audience for her story and told it all over again to

anyone on the bus who would listen. At the next stop, Penelope's best friend, Trudi, got on, so she had to be told, too. Left alone, Annie smiled quietly to herself, ate her sandwich, and made up an exciting story to keep herself awake.

In it, she and Ned soared over Pebbles's blue barrels — at last.